W9-CNZ-957

ON

MADELINE IN LONDON

Books About Madeline

Madeline
Madeline and the Bad Hat
Madeline and the Gypsies
Madeline in London
Madeline's Christmas
Madeline's Rescue

MADELINE
IN
London

by

Ludwig Bemelmans

PUFFIN BOOKS

PUFFIN BOOKS
Published by the Penguin Group
Penguin Putnam Books for Young Readers, 345 Hudson Street, New York, New York 10014, U.S.A.
Penguin Books Ltd, 27 Wrights Lane, London W8 5TZ, England
Penguin Books Australia Ltd, Ringwood, Victoria, Australia
Penguin Books Canada Ltd, 10 Alcorn Avenue, Toronto, Ontario, Canada M4V 3B2
Penguin Books (N.Z.) Ltd, 182-190 Wairau Road, Auckland 10, New Zealand

Penguin Books Ltd, Registered Offices: Harmondsworth, Middlesex, England

First published by The Viking Press, 1961
Viking Seafarer edition, 1972
Published in Puffin Books, 1977
Reissued by Puffin Books, division of Penguin Putnam Books for Young Readers, 2000

Copyright © Ludwig, Bemelmans, 1961
Copyright © renewed Madeline Bemelmans and Barbara Bemelmans Marciano, 1989
All rights reserved

ISBN 978-1-61129-449-1

Printed at Phoenix Color
Rockaway, N.J.
February 2011

Except in the United States of America, this book is sold subject to the condition that it shall not,
by way of trade or otherwise, be lent, re-sold, hired out, or otherwise circulated without the publisher's
prior consent in any form of binding or cover other than that in which it is published and without
a similar condition including this condition being imposed on the subsequent purchaser.

**In an old house
in Paris**

**that was covered
with vines**

**Lived twelve little girls
in two straight lines.**

They left the house

at half past nine.

**The smallest one
was Madeline.**

**In another old house
that stood next door**

**Lived Pepito,
the son of**

the Spanish Ambassador.

**An Ambassador doesn't
have to pay rent,
But he has to move
to wherever he's sent.**

**He took his family
and his hat;**

**They left for England—
all but the cat.**

"I'm glad," said the cat.
"There goes that bad hat.
Let him annoy some other kitten
At the Embassy in Great Britain."
The little girls all cried: "Boo-hoo—
We'd like to go to London too"

In London Pepito just picked at his dinner,
Soon he grew thin and then he grew thinner—

And when he began to look like a stick
His mama said, "My, this boy looks sick.
I think Pepito is lonely for
Madeline and the little girls next door."

His papa called Paris. "Hello, Miss Clavel,
My little Pepito is not at all well.

"He misses you; and he's lonesome for
Madeline and the little girls next door.

"May we request the pleasure of your company—
There's plenty of room here at our embassy."

"Quick, darlings, pack your bags, and we'll get
Out to the airport and catch the next jet."

Fill the house with lovely flowers,

Fly our flags from all the towers.

For Pepito's birthday bake
The most wonderful birthday cake.

Place twelve beds in two straight lines.
The last one here will be Madeline's.

"Welcome to London, the weather's fine,
And it's exactly half past nine."

"Good Heavens," said Miss Clavel, "we've brought no toy
For his excellency's little boy!"
Said Madeline, "Everybody knows, of course,
He always said he craved a horse."
In their little purses and in Miss Clavel's bag
There wasn't enough money to buy the meanest nag.

But in London there's a place to get
A retired horse to keep as a pet.

And when they went to the place, they found
A horse that was gentle, strong, and sound.

Some poor old dobbins are made into glue,
But not this one—

Look, he's as good as new.

"Happy birthday, Pepito, happy birthday to you.

This lovely horse belongs to you."

Just then—"Tara, tara"—a trumpet blew
Suddenly outside, and off he flew
Over the wall to take his place at the head

Of the Queen's Life Guards, which he had always led
Before the Royal Society for the Protection of Horses
Had retired him from Her Majesty's Forces.

"Oh, dear! They've gone. Oh, what a pity!

Come, children, we'll find them in the city."

"Careful, girls, watch your feet.

Look right before you cross the street."

Oh, for a cup of tea and crumpets—

Hark, hark, there goes the sound of trumpets.

These birds have seen

all this before.

But they are glad

of an encore.

And so are the people—on ship...

and shore.

And now it's getting really grand.

Here comes the mascot and his band.

The people below are stout and loyal,

And those on the balcony mostly Royal.

The show is over, it's getting dark
In the city, in the park.
Dinner is waiting; we must be on time.
Now let's find Pepito and Madeline.

Well, isn't it lovely—they're standing sentry
Right here at the Whitehall entry.
That is the power and the beauty:
In England everyone does his duty!

Visiting is fun and gay—

Let's celebrate a lovely day.

Everyone had been well fed,

Everyone was in his bed.

Only one was forgotten, he'd been on his feet
All day long, without anything to eat.

In a cottage that was thatched,
Wearing trousers that were patched,
Lived the gardener, who loved flowers,
Especially in the morning hours,
When their faces, fresh with dew,
Smiled at him—"How DO you do?"

The gardener, who was never late,
Opened up the garden gate.

The gardener dropped his garden hose.

There wasn't a daisy or a rose.

"All my work and all my care
For nought! Oh, this is hard to bear.

"Where's my celery, carrots, tomatoes, my beans and peas?
And not an apple on my apple trees!"

Everybody had to cry.
Not a single eye was dry.

Oh, look who is lying there,
With his feet up in the air.

"I feel his breath, he's not dead yet.
Quick, Pepito, get the vet."

The vet said, "Don't worry, he's only asleep.
Help me get him on his feet.

"As a diet, there is nothing worse
Than green apples and roses for an old horse."
"Dear lady," said Miss Clavel, "we beg your pardon.
It seems our horse has eaten up your garden.

"A little sunshine, a little rain,
And it all will be the same again."
Pepito's mother said, "Quite so, quite so!
Still I'm afraid the horse must go."

Then Madeline cried, "I know what to do.
Pepito, let us take care of him for you."

"Fasten your seat belts, in half an hour
You will see the Eiffel Tower."

"Madeline, Madeline, where have you been?"
"We've been to London to see the Queen."

"At last," sighed Madeline, "we are able
To sit down without being thirteen at table."

They brushed his teeth and gave him bread,

And covered him up

and put him to bed.

"Good night, little girls,

Thank the Lord you are well.

And now go to sleep," said Miss Clavel.

And she turned out the light and closed the door.

There were twelve upstairs, and below one more.